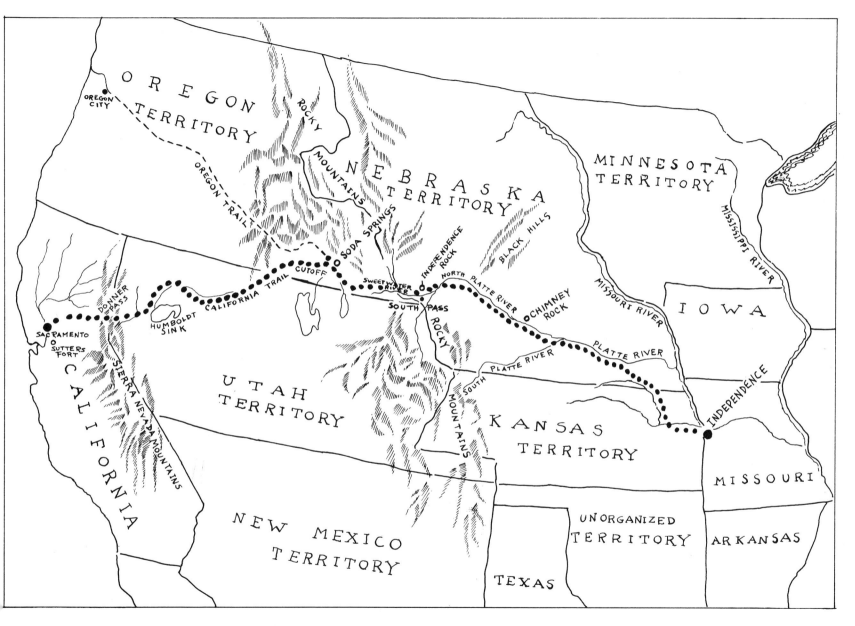

Cassie's Journey

by Brett Harvey
illustrated by Deborah Kogan Ray

CASSIE'S JOURNEY
Going West in the 1860s

Holiday House / New York

For my brother Jan
B.H.

For Naomi and Bill
D.K.R.

Text copyright © 1988 by Brett Harvey
Illustrations copyright © 1988 by Deborah Kogan
Printed in the United States of America
All rights reserved
First Edition

Library of Congress Cataloging-in-Publication Data
Harvey, Brett.
Cassie's journey.

SUMMARY: A young girl relates the hardships and
dangers of traveling with her family in a covered wagon
from Illinois to California during the 1860's.
[1. Overland journeys to the Pacific—Fiction.
2. Frontier and pioneer life—Fiction.   3. West (U.S.)—
Fiction]   1. Ray, Deborah, ill.   II. Title.
PZ7.H26747Cas 1988   [E]   87-23599
ISBN 0-8234-0684-9

From 1840 to 1870, a remarkable event took place in America: a quarter of a million people uprooted themselves and migrated westward across the continent. From Maine to Kansas, whole families, as well as individual men and women, sold their possessions, piled into covered wagons, and began the long trek west. Today, when we can fly from Illinois to California in a few hours, it's difficult to imagine that the same journey could have taken six to eight months full of danger and hardship. Why did they go? Many, like the family in this book, left home because it was too hard to farm in the harsh midwestern climate. Some were lured by the promise of veins of gold in the western mountains, and some went for the sheer adventure of it.

We know what their journeys were like today because so many of the pioneers—especially the women—kept diaries. We may imagine such a woman, crouched by the firelight, her children sleeping safely in the wagon, scribbling her record of the day's events: how many miles traveled, how many rivers crossed, how hungry or thirsty they were, the trees and rocks, flowers and animals they saw along the way; the death of a beloved child from a snakebite.

Everything in this book is based on actual accounts, many of which came from *Women's Diaries of the Westward Journey* by Lillian Schliffel.

BRETT HARVEY
July 15, 1987

We're on our way to California! I'm riding up high with Papa, and the wind is rocking the wagon. When I look back I can see a long line of wagons curling behind us like a snake in the dust.

At home in Illinois we had a farm, but things weren't going so well. We couldn't sell our wheat for enough money and some of our harvest was ruined in a drought. Then we got a letter from Mama's sister Rose, who went to live in California three years ago. She said it's always warm there and you can grow things all year round. Land is cheap and there's lots of it. Right away Papa wanted to go. Mama wasn't so sure. She said "It's too far and the trip is too hard and how do we know what we'll find?" But Papa told her we didn't have anything to look forward to in Illinois except cold in the winter and fever in the summer. He said we should take a chance on a new life in a new place. And finally Mama agreed.

So we sold our farm and said good-bye to everybody. Mama and I cried till our eyes ached when we had to leave Aunt Irene and Grandma and all our friends.

Now this wagon is our home. Papa made it strong enough to cross mountains and go over rivers. Our wagon is 10 feet wide and 15 feet long, and it's covered with two thicknesses of canvas to make it waterproof in the rain. The wagon box is blue with *Zephyrus* painted on the front in big letters. That was Papa's idea—it means "west wind" in Latin. Papa loves the Greeks and Romans—"the ancients," he calls them. He named us all after them.

Inside, it's cozy and snug. On the bottom of the wagon is our hair mattress covered with feather beds and quilts. Mama sewed pockets along the sides of the canvas to hold our most important things: our *Bible*, some quinine in case we get the fever, and a bottle of citric acid to keep us from getting scurvy because of not being able to eat fresh fruit or vegetables. Most important of all, we store our matches in a jar with a tight cap that keeps them dry. Mama even made a special pocket for my doll Hettie.

We've brought flour, sugar, rice and bacon, dried meat and vegetables, yeast, vinegar, and gallon jugs of wild plum and blackberry jam. We have four oxen to pull our wagon, and our milk cow Portia. Our dog Cato is going to be our watchdog.

Before we left, Papa and Mama sat my brother Plato and me down for a talk. They said we will have to work even harder than at home. Mama said we wouldn't have time for regular schooling, but that she'd try to squeeze in a lesson here and there.

There are twelve wagons in our caravan. Almost all are owned by families with children and dogs. The grown-ups keep talking about "seeing the elephant." That's when you want to turn back and go home. I'm sure *I* won't see the elephant!

We get up at five o'clock in the morning, because the wagon train moves out at six, and no family wants their wagon to be the last in the caravan. Mama and I make breakfast on an open fire. The smoke stings my eyes, and some days the wind blows so hard we can hardly get the fire lit. Today Mama's bonnet almost blew into the flames. We have pancakes or bread and bacon and coffee for breakfast.

We have to travel between fifteen and twenty miles a day if we want to reach Independence Rock by the Fourth of July. We've heard that if you don't reach Independence Rock by then, you might get trapped in the mountains later when the snow comes.

Mama rides in the wagon, but my brother Plato and I like to walk behind it until we get tired. Our job is to pick up buffalo chips. There isn't enough wood on the prairie, so we use chips for our fire. If I turn in a circle, I see a carpet of flowers of every color all around me. The sunbonnet Mama makes me wear flaps in the wind, and the wild geese sing high in the sky above us.

When it starts to get dark, the wagon master finds our camping place, and we all turn in, one wagon going to the right, the next to the left, until the wagons are in a big circle. Then everyone piles out of the wagons. The younger children run around and play, but we older ones have to work. Plato gets to help Papa water and feed the animals and put up the tents. I have to help Mama make the fire and cook supper. I wish I were Plato. I hate to cook.

It's been raining for two days and everything is wet, wet, wet—our clothes, our bedding, even our food. Last night the rain was so heavy and the wind was blowing so hard that we couldn't make a fire. We had cold coffee and soggy bread for supper. This morning Mama cooked our breakfast under an umbrella. Today it's raining in sheets of gray so we have to stay in the wagon with the flaps tied down tight. I hate riding in the wagon—its swaying motion and the screeching noise of the wheels make me feel seasick. Mama is drilling us in our multiplication tables. I wonder if we'll ever be dry again.

Now we are dry as dust and hard as bones and all we think about is water. We are following along the Platte River, and sometimes I want to throw myself in and drink it all up. But the Platte has a bad taste, and Mama warned us not to drink it because people are getting sick and dying from the water. Papa says Platte means "flat," and that the Platte is "too thin to plow, too thick to drink, and too muddy to bathe in." We still have plenty of water in our rain barrel, but Papa says it has to last us a long time. We can only have two cups a day. Even the wheels of our wagon will dry out if we don't take them off every night and soak them in the river. There are mosquitoes, too—so many they even got in the bread dough and turned it gray. Plato and I wouldn't eat it at first, but then we got so hungry we had to.

Mama must drive today because Papa's feeling sickly. I rolled out a piecrust on the wagon seat this morning, with Mama telling me how to do it. Mama and I discovered that if we keep the butter churn on the seat, the bouncing of the wagon makes delicious butter and buttermilk by the end of the day.

We're passing hills that have strange and wonderful shapes. They look like cities, with castles and temples all made of rock. I went and pulled back the canvas so that Papa could see, too.

I have a new friend named Alice Dealey. She and her family come from Iowa, and they're bound for Oregon. Yesterday evening Alice and I went in search of buffalo chips for the fire. We were so busy talking we didn't notice how far we'd gone from the wagons. All of a sudden we felt the earth rumble under our feet. We looked up to see a low, black mountain approaching us at top speed—buffalo! A whole herd in a cloud of dust, their noses to the ground, tails flying, snorting wildly. Suddenly something grabbed me off my feet and the next thing I knew I was flying through the air under someone's arm, and then, thud! I was thrown flat on the ground with my face in the dust. When the thundering noise was over, I picked my head up and saw Mama and Mrs. Dealey running toward us. They were crying and laughing at the same time. After the dust finally settled, we saw what had happened to a wagon that had been in the path of the stampede. There was nothing left of it but a pile of sticks. Papa had seen the buffalo coming just in time to save us.

On this trip we see many, many graves—some of them are no more than wooden crosses with signs on them stuck in the dirt. Alice and I have been counting and so far, we've seen thirty-one. We always read the signs and think about the people who died. Especially the children. One said "Here lies Eliza Harris. Born July 7 1840, died July 1 1843 from falling out of her family's wagon." Another sign said "Here lize our onlee son, John Hanna, bit by a snake at 7 years of age." There are so many dangers on this journey. It makes me shiver to think of all the narrow escapes we've already had, and we're not yet near the end of our journey.

All week we've been waiting to cross the Platte, but the river has been dangerously high and fast moving. Last night the wagon master called us together and told us if we waited any longer to cross, we might not get through the mountains before the snows come. So we made our preparations. The wheels had to be taken off all the wagons, and the canvas wrapped tight around their boxes to keep everything dry. First the men and the older boys pulled the boxes across the river with ropes they'd tied around their bodies. Then Mama, Plato and I, along with the other women and children, were pulled across the river by the men, in the bottom of an empty wagon box. I kept my eyes squeezed shut and held on to Mama for dear life while our "boat" lurched and bumped and the water roared in my ears.

Finally the men began swimming the oxen and other livestock across. While Papa was taking Portia across, the rope slipped off her horn and the current carried her away downstream. Papa tried to go after her, but the current was too strong. We think she must have drowned. Poor Portia. And poor us—no more fresh milk for the rest of the trip.

Today we reached Independence Rock a week early. It looks like a huge turtle rising out of the plain. Papa took Plato and Alice and me to the top. From here we can see the Rocky Mountains in the distance. There are hundreds of names carved into the sides of the rock by travelers who came before us. We carved ours there, too. I like to think of people who come after us reading what we've written and wondering about us.

We're camped on the banks of the beautiful Sweetwater River. Even its name is nicer than the Platte. We are resting here for two whole days. Mama and I washed our clothes in the river this morning and spread them on rocks to dry. Papa caught us some fish for supper. Tomorrow is the Sabbath, and Mama is happy because we will honor it for the first time on this journey by not traveling.

Even though it's a week too soon, we decided to celebrate the Fourth of July at Independence Rock. We all put on our best clothes and made a big bonfire in the middle of the wagon circle. Some of the men played their fiddles and Papa danced a jig with Mama. It made me giggle and feel funny to see them dance together. We sang *Oh Susanna!* and lots of other songs, and the older boys fired their guns in the air. Mama let us stay up till after midnight—the latest I've ever been up!

Today we saw our first Indians! We're camped on the Sweetwater River at South Pass now—it's called that because the easiest place to pass through the Rocky Mountains is in the south. When the Indians first came into camp at sunset, we were all frightened because they looked so strange. They wore soft animal skins with beads and feathers sewn onto them. But they let us know they didn't mean to hurt us, only to trade with us. We gave them calico cloth and bread in return for moccasins and buffalo meat. I hate buffalo meat because it's too chewy.

Alice's mother has been very sick with fever, and this morning she died. Papa and Mr. Dealey made a coffin out of a wagon box. The men dug a deep, deep hole for her grave and then piled stones on top of it so that the wolves wouldn't dig it up. There's no minister in the caravan, and we didn't have time for a real funeral, but we sang *Nearer My God to Thee* over her grave, and then we moved on.

Now we are really in the mountains. The paths are so steep and slippery that the wagons tip and sway, and it's too dangerous to ride in them. Every step we take sends a shower of loose stones down the mountainside. Along the path we see things people had to leave behind to lighten their loads—chairs, bedsteads, chests, barrels. Even our load was too heavy, and we had to leave Mama's china, her rocking chair, and Papa's books. Pulling the wagon up the side of a mountain takes all our strength. But coming down is even worse because we have to keep the wagon from going too fast and crushing the animals. We tie young pine trees to the axle so that the branches will slow the wagon.

Here we are at Soda Springs, where the water bubbles up out of the ground at a boil. Alice and I tried to make our tea by holding our cups under the geyser, but the tea tasted funny.

Tomorrow, Alice and I must say good-bye. She and her family go north to the Oregon Trail, while we turn south toward California. She and I have become almost like sisters. How sad it is to think that we may never see each other again. Tonight we were crying so hard while we washed the supper dishes we could barely see them.

We've finally come through the mountains, and how I wish we were back in them. This place we're in now is by far the worst place we've traveled. It's called the Humboldt Sink, and it's a kind of desert with few trees and not much grass for the animals to eat. But the worst of it is the alkali dust—a kind of white dust that burns your nose and eyes and throat. We are running low on water, too, and think about it constantly. We have used up most of our food except for flour, so most nights all we have for supper is biscuits and watery gravy unless Papa has shot a bird for us to eat. How much I would love a juicy piece of buffalo meat now! Because there are no trees and no buffalo here, we have no fuel for a fire. One night we burned the wood from a wagon we found abandoned by the side of the trail. What happened to the family that lived in that wagon, I wonder?

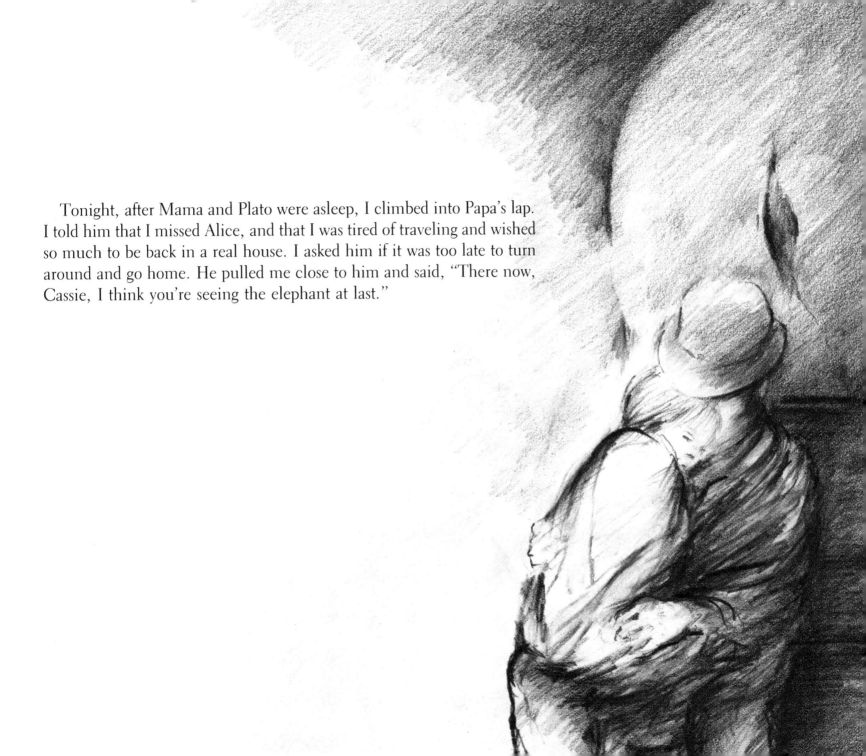

Tonight, after Mama and Plato were asleep, I climbed into Papa's lap. I told him that I missed Alice, and that I was tired of traveling and wished so much to be back in a real house. I asked him if it was too late to turn around and go home. He pulled me close to him and said, "There now, Cassie, I think you're seeing the elephant at last."

We're in the mountains again—this time, the Sierra Nevadas. These mountains are the hardest we've had to cross. Today a rope broke and one of the wagons went crashing down the mountainside, with pots and pans and bedding flying through the air and landing far below. No one was hurt, but the family lost everything they owned. Mama and I took them a pot to cook in and some blankets. Last night it was so cold the water froze in the pail. We had to sleep in the wagon all huddled up together to keep warm. Papa says we must pray the snows don't come early.

Today when I was riding up with Papa, we came 'round a mountain and suddenly, spread out far below us, was a soft green valley, like a velvety carpet with little hills under it. Papa says that's where we're going. We still have to go down the other side of these terrible mountains, and Papa says we have yet another river to cross. But now I can close my eyes and see a picture of that green valley, and imagine Aunt Rose and her family waiting for us in a little house with windows and doors that sits still on the ground and doesn't go anywhere. Now I know we're going to get there!